THERE WAS AN OLD LADY WHO SWALLOWED A BELL!

by Lucille Colandro
Illustrated by Jared Lee

SCHOLASTIC INC.

For Marietta and Mia, who love Christmas
— L.C.

To Ginger Estepp,
longtime dedicated associate
— J.L.

ISBN 978-1-338-32019-0

Text copyright © 2006 by Lucille Colandro.
Illustrations copyright © 2006 by Jared D. Lee Studio, Inc.
All rights reserved. Published by Scholastic Inc. SCHOLASTIC, CARTWHEEL BOOKS, and associated logos are trademarks and/or registered trademarks of Scholastic Inc.

10 9 8 7 6 5 4 3 2 1   18 19 20 21 22

Made in Jiaxing City, China   68

First printing, November 2006

This edition first printing 2018

There was an old lady who swallowed a bell.
How it jingled and jangled and tickled, as well!
I don't know why she swallowed a bell.
I wish she'd tell.

There was an old lady who swallowed some bows.
Soft as the snow, were those velvety bows.

She swallowed the bows to tie up the bell
that jingled and jangled and tickled, as well!

I don't know why she swallowed a bell.
I wish she'd tell.

There was an old lady who swallowed some gifts.
It gave her a lift to swallow the gifts.

She swallowed the gifts to go with the bows.
She swallowed the bows to tie up the bell
that jingled and jangled and tickled, as well!
I don't know why she swallowed a bell. I wish she'd tell.

There was an old lady who swallowed a sack.
It was easy to pack—a very big sack.

She swallowed the sack to hold all the gifts.
She swallowed the gifts to go with the bows.

She swallowed the bows to tie up the bell
that jingled and jangled and tickled, as well!
I don't know why she swallowed a bell. I wish she'd tell.

There was an old lady who swallowed a sleigh.
What a ton it weighed, that shiny red sleigh!

She swallowed the sleigh to carry the sack.

She swallowed the sack to hold all the gifts.

She swallowed the gifts to go with the bows.
She swallowed the bows to tie up the bell
that jingled and jangled and tickled, as well!

I don't know why she swallowed a bell.
I wish she'd tell.

There was an old lady who swallowed some reindeer.
They were in full flight gear, those soaring reindeer.

She swallowed the reindeer to steer the sleigh.

She swallowed the sleigh to carry the sack.

She swallowed the sack to hold all the gifts.

She swallowed the gifts to go with the bows.

She swallowed the bows to tie up the bell
that jingled and jangled and tickled, as well!
I don't know why she swallowed a bell. I wish she'd tell.

Then the old lady needed a treat.
She thought a candy cane would be very sweet.

But when she heard a jolly "Ho! Ho! Ho!"
She knew it was time for her to go.

So she whistled loudly and soon by her side . . .

... was Santa Claus waiting for a ride!

Happy holidays to all!